Mr Tripsy's
Boat Trip

Brian Leo Lee

ISBN 978-1484912034

About the Author

The author was born in Manchester. On leaving school, a period in accountancy was followed by a teaching career in Primary Education.
He is the writer of several children's short stories including the popular Bouncey the Elf series.
Now retired and living in South Yorkshire.

As Brian Leo Lee
(Children's stories)
Just Bouncey
Bouncey the Elf and Friends Meet Again
Bouncey the Elf and Friends Together Again
Mr Tripsy's Trip

As Brian Leon Lee
Trimefirst

All available as eBooks

www.bounceytheelf.co.uk

For
Karen and Stephen

Chapter 1

Mr Tripsy gave a big yawn and stretched his arms. *Aaaah! Should I do it though?* he wondered. He was sitting in his armchair, in his small living room with a strange looking map on his knees. It was covered with lots of blue wiggly lines; many of them marked with little v shapes. Funny names like Shugbrough Lock, Chells Aqueduct, Ivy House Lift Bridge and Cowroast Moorings were dotted about it as well.

Leaning over the edge of his armchair he stroked his cat Flapjax, who was sprawled comfortably in front of the gas fire, gently behind one of his ears. Flapjax rolled onto his back and purred for a moment or two before returning to his interrupted dream of eating a supply of unlimited Fishio sticks.

'Well, thanks very much,' said Mr Tripsy with a grin as he looked down at Flapjax. 'I was just about to tell you that I had decided to book my next holiday and no, it will not be caravan trip either.'

He gave a little shudder as he remembered that mini break with his new folding caravan. It nearly turned into a disaster, so many mishaps.

This time though, things would be different. He had decided to book a few days holiday on a canal. *Yes,* he thought. *What could go wrong on a canal trip?*

He looked at the map again. He had read the bit about what the v shapes and other symbols on the map meant. A v or vvv meant one or more sets of canal lock gates. The gates opened and shut, either letting water in or out of the lock.

I know one thing, thought Mr Tripsy, looking at his map. *You won't be able to rush up and down a canal if you*

have to keep stopping to open and close all those lock gates.
Anyway, the whole idea is to have a quiet, relaxing trip.

———

Chapter 2

'Nearly there,' Mr Tripsy called over his shoulder, as he turned a corner into Western Flash Marina and gave a quick glance at Flapjax who was now beginning to feel the effects of their long journey.

Flapjax sat up in his basket, which was firmly attached to the rear seat and looked out of the side window at a row of assorted boats moored alongside the towpath of a canal. *Caravans on water,* he thought. *Will he never learn?*

"Well, it doesn't look too bad does it,' exclaimed Mr Tripsy as he got out of the car. 'I'll be back in a jiffy,' he said walking to the reception office.

Twenty minutes later he returned carrying a large plastic folder. 'Look at all this bumph,' he said, waving the folder at Flapjax. 'I mean, who needs all this stuff?'

Flapjax sniffed the air and waved his tail. *Oh Oh,* he thought. *Here we go again. The expert of everything and the master of nothing.*

'Once I have parked the car we can go on board 'Wave Crest,' explained Mr Tripsy as he backed out of the reception area.

'Hey! Watch where you're going!' An angry shout from behind Mr Tripsy made him brake hurriedly.

A large red-headed man was leaning out of the driving window of a large 4x4, which had stopped just behind Mr Tripsy's car. 'You should be wearing specks, idiot.'

Mr Tripsy leant out of his car window and said, 'Sorry, I really didn't see you and I already wear glasses.'

Now Mr Tripsy was not a tall man, or small for that matter.

His hair was blondish and spiky. On his rather long nose, a good feature he thought, his thick-framed pair of glasses often fought gravity to stay there. His face often gave the impression that he was frowning, upset with something, but that was just the way he was.

Actually, he was a quiet, friendly person and he was wearing his holiday clothes which included a natty Breton sailing cap and a bright orange coloured T-shirt with the logo 'Ahoy Captain' printed in large purple letters.

'Well, you need to get a new pair,' snapped the red-headed man. 'Now let me past before you do anything else stupid.' With a clunk of gears, a racing engine and with a cloud of belching black smoke from his exhaust, he drove off to the other end of the marina.

'What a ....' said Mr Tripsy calmly. 'I suppose it takes all sorts.'

Making sure that no one was behind him, he reversed slowly out and then made his way to the long stay car park.

It only took him ten minutes or so to transfer his luggage, plus a box of food for both of them and of course Flapjax with his basket and litter tray and stuff, to the sleek looking cabin cruiser 'Wave Crest.'

'Wow! I didn't expect this.' Mr Tripsy was nearly speechless as he examined the inside cabin.

A sumptuous L shaped settee with a fold away table, fitted carpets, TV, separate sleeping cabin with shower and a galley (kitchen). A raised area at the front of the main cabin contained the cockpit, with a sliding bench seat set to one side of it (most captains stood whilst steering). Then the steering wheel and the bright and shiny control panel.

He decided to make a cup of hot chocolate once he had fed Flapjax, who as always, looked for a place to nap after he had had a meal. He found it. Just above the steering wheel was a ledge and he at once settled on it. Flapjax had noticed that he had a great view forward through the boat's windscreen and satisfied for the moment, he began to doze off.

Meanwhile, Mr Tripsy had begun to make his cup of hot chocolate. The kettle was just beginning to boil when the boat began to rock and heave about quite violently.

'What the…!' cried Mr Tripsy as he quickly grabbed a safety rail. He looked out of a side window and saw a canal narrow boat rushing by, going far too fast for the marina, which was a restricted speed area. At the rudder was the red-headed man who had argued with him a short time ago. He saw Mr Tripsy looking through the window and just grinned. By his side a tiny Yorkshire terrier, with its front paws on the narrow boat's gunnel, was barking its head off as though it was aping its master.

Chapter 3

Feeling much better after his hot drink, Mr Tripsy had a quick look at the engine manual and returned it to the slot on the left of the steering wheel, being careful not to wake Flapjax.

He then sat down behind the steering wheel and reached out towards the ignition key. He jerked his hand back. *Get on with it. It won't bite,* he said to himself. So he reached out again and turned on the engine.

At once Wave Crest's hull began to vibrate and shudder. Flapjax shot up with a screech of alarm and jumped off the cockpit ledge. *Just like a scalded cat,* thought Mr Tripsy with a smile, before realizing that it wasn't really funny at all and switched off the engine. Flapjax had run to his basket and was standing stiffly inside it, his eyes rolling wildly.

The sudden quiet and the stopping of the vibration through the hull, calmed Flapjax down enough for him to be picked up by Mr Tripsy, who, by stroking and speaking quietly and with the offer of a couple of Fishio sticks soon had Flapjax fully relaxed again and he began to explore the boat.

He suddenly had a horrible thought, *What if Flapjax couldn't adapt to the boat, especially when under power. Why didn't I think of that before? What can I do?*

Then he had an idea. He rounded up Flapjax and put him on the cockpit ledge just above the steering wheel. Keeping one hand on Flapjax's back, he started the boat engine and then quickly turned it off.

Flapjax's body twitched and he tried to jump off the ledge but was restrained by Mr Tripsy's hand.

For the next twenty minutes it was engine on, engine off and all the while Mr Tripsy spoke in a quietly and gently soothing voice, saying that everything would be alright. It worked.

Flapjax soon stopped flinching at the start of the engine and the vibration that followed. He actually began to look through the cockpit windscreen and take an interest in the goings on in the marina.

'Phew!' gasped a very relieved Mr Tripsy. 'I thought for a minute that I would have to cancel my boating holiday.'

Not wanting to waste any more time, he patted Flapjax on the back for good luck and started the engine. He put the engine clutch to forward and gently eased the throttle a notch. Wave Crest began to move then jerked to a stop. 'What's wrong,' said Mr Tripsy in a worried voice.

He suddenly noticed several people on the marina, shouting and pointing at the boat. Not knowing what was going on, Mr Tripsy pulled the throttle back and putting the clutch to neutral, stopped the engine. Now he could hear the shouting.

'Your mooring lines! Your mooring lines! They're still tied.'

'Oh! Oh!' said Mr Tripsy anxiously. 'What have I done?'

The Manager of the marina came running up to the side of Wave Crest waving his arms wildly.

Mr Tripsy slid a side window open.

'What on earth are you doing?' the Marina Manager stuttered. He was out of breath after rushing from his office. 'Didn't you check your mooring lines?'

'I…. I….' Mr Tripsy was lost for words. 'I sort of forgot.'

'Forgot!' cried the Marina Manager. 'Forgot! How can you forget to remove your mooring lines?'

'I'm very sorry. It won't happen again, I promise.'

'Well, fortunately for you no damage was done, so we'll let it go this time. Make sure you check the mooring every time, OK.'

Mr Tripsy waited until every one had gone and with one last look round, untied the stern line and after releasing the bowline, jumped quickly aboard Wave Crest and started the engine. Then, clutch to forward, he gently eased the throttle one notch. Wave Crest began to move forward and with a slight turn of the steering wheel, Mr Tripsy guided the boat towards the marina's exit.

His boating holiday had really begun.

Chapter 4

Mr Tripsy entered the waterway full of excitement. Here he was, captain of Wave Crest, cruising down the River Weaver. *Strange,* he thought, *to begin a canal holiday on a river. But this was the quickest way to get into this part of the canal system especially if you wanted to explore this area of the country. So here I am.*

Looking downstream he saw that the riverbanks were mostly wooded and in places branches hung out over the river. *Must keep an eye out for things like that*, he muttered to himself.

Suddenly, the boat started to swing towards the left side of the river. Closer and closer to the riverbank went Wave Crest. With a jerk, he spun the steering wheel. Not being used to the 'feel' of the boat's reactions to a course correction, (after all, he had been captain for all of about fifteen minutes), the boat began to veer sharply to the opposite side of the river. *Keep calm, he said to himself. Keep calm. Remember the boating hints in the handbook.*

Ah, yes. Think before you act. Good idea but what about how to stop the boat crashing into the riverbank?

Mr Tripsy looked anxiously around. Fortunately no other boat was in sight, so he gave the steering wheel another twitch and sighed in relief as the boat eased back into the center of the river. As he thought of what he had just done, the steering wheel began to jerk and twist in his hands. 'What the…' he exclaimed in amazement, and then he realized that the boat's rudder must be being affected by a river current.

Of course, he thought. *I remember now. In a river you need to keep up a good speed or the river current could knock you off course. That's what's just happened*

He looked down at Flapjax snoozing as usual on the cockpit ledge and grinned. 'See I told you it wouldn't be difficult.'

Flapjax opened one eye and thought, *Famous last words.*

Now feeling pretty confident, Mr Tripsy increased speed by pushing the throttle forwards another notch.

He felt even better when the sun came out and the river sparkled where ripples and eddies of water reflected the sunbeams brightly in a variety of colours and hues. Then a kingfisher darted to and fro before diving in the river and appearing a moment later with a twitching minnow between its beak.

'Wow! This is brilliant,' he marvelled.

Then the river began to curve and Mr Tripsy took a quick glance at the map, blue-tacked on the side window, next to the cockpit. 'I reckon we're near the boat lift,' he said, looking down at Flapjax who by now was beginning to stir and take notice of his surroundings.

Rounding the river bend Mr Tripsy's mouth dropped wide-open. He was gob smacked. The sight of the Anderton Boat Lift took his breath away.

He had read about it of course but this was different. It was amazing, perched on the banks of the River Weaver like some giant iron spider. He knew it was built in 1875 to lift cargo boats the 50 feet from the River Weaver to the Trent & Mersey Canal. Two huge water tanks, each with watertight sealable doors carry the boats up and down, using a counterbalanced system of weights. And it only took three minutes to lift them.

Approaching the boat lift, Mr Tripsy was pleased to see that there was only one other boat waiting to use it. (It took two at a time normally).

However, he had forgotten about the river current.

He eased back the throttle to slow down and turned the steering wheel in order to glide in towards the boat lift entrance. (The watergates were already open and the other boat was inching its way into one of them).

Without any warning, the bow (front) of Wave Crest began to swing round and the boat was now moving down river, carried by the current.

'Oh Sugar!' cried out Mr Tripsy in alarm. As quickly as he could he pushed the throttle up two notches and the extra speed gave him control of the boat again. He straightened up the bow and was just about to turn the boat about when a canal narrow boat passed by going upriver. It gave a *toot, toot,* as it passed and looking over he was amazed to see the red-headed man from the marina.

'Having a good day,' shouted the man and he laughed loudly as he guided his narrow boat towards the boat lift watergates.

'I don't believe it! He's going to take my place,' said an annoyed Mr Tripsy as he finished the turn and went to tie up at the parking buoy bobbing next to the boat lift entrances. He watched in frustration as the boat lift took the two boats up to the top level.

It wasn't too long before he too was able to enter the boat lift. The water level of the river matched the level in the giant lift tank, so, inching in, very slowly, he hardly moved the throttle, making sure not to catch the boat's side against the metal sides of the boat lift, (he had fortunately remembered to put the boat fenders in place first) and stopped the engine.

A few minutes later he was fifty feet higher in the world and he was easing Wave Crest into the Trent and Mersey Canal. 'That was fantastic,' he said, giving Flapjax a friendly pat.

Flapjax look round at him, as if to say. *Can we celebrate with some Fishio sticks?*

Chapter 5

As he sailed along the canal Mr Tripsy noticed a couple of things that were different to being on the River Weaver. Being manmade, the canal is narrower and has straighter banks than the river, usually with a towpath on one side (in earlier times horses were used to pull the boats) and there is no river current to worry about. This point in particular, pleased him no end. It was so much easier to steer the boat on a canal.

So making sure to stay in the middle, he tootled along at a steady but slow speed. He passed through a cutting. (If a large hill was in the way the canal route was taking, a *'cut'* was dug through it.) The sides of this cutting were so high and steep that in places it got quite dark. (Sometimes, small landslips, including rocks would tumble down into the canal.)

Chugging into the sunlight, Mr Tripsy relaxed, glad to be out of the gloomy *'cut'*. It came as a shock when a set of locks suddenly came into view.

Quickly recovering, he reduced speed and then put the clutch to neutral as he throttled back to idle speed. Wave Crest slowed to a stop just before the lock gates.

'On your own?' a friendly voice called from the side of the lock. It was the lock keeper. He asked for the bowline, so Mr Tripsy had to leave the cockpit and get the coiled rope lying on the front deck. He threw the line to the lock keeper who caught it deftly and tied it to a mooring ring. 'Hang on while I empty the lock. Someone has just gone through and I was just about to do it.'

Mr Tripsy watched very carefully. He might have to do this on his own later on.

The lock keeper walked over to the lock gate and picked up a winding handle called a windlass.

Mr Tripsy knew that one like it was clipped to the side of the cockpit and had wondered what it was for.

Fixing it to a winding wheel attached to the top of the lock gate the lock keeper began to turn it. A jet of water suddenly spurted out of the lock gate just near the bottom of it. A large piece of the gate (called a paddle) was slowly being raised up, allowing the water inside the lock to be released. The jet got bigger and a torrent of water rushed down the canal, passing by Wave Crest, which bobbed and twisted, on the end of its bowline.

'Wow,' exclaimed an excited Mr Tripsy. 'It's a good job we were tied up.'

In a short while, the water inside of the lock was the same level to that outside, where Wave Crest was waiting.

The lock keeper then opened the lock gate by pushing the balance beam (the huge, long piece of timber sticking out from the lock gate, usually painted white). He then untied the bowline from the mooring ring and signalled to Mr Tripsy to enter the lock.

So Mr Tripsy nervously put the clutch to forward and eased the throttle a notch and slowly guided Wave Crest into the lock. The lock keeper then closed the lock gate and lowered the gate paddle, again using the windlass, after making sure that the bowline was tied to another mooring ring further up the lock.

Once the bottom paddle was safely down, the lock keeper took the windlass off the winding wheel and took it to the gate at the other end of the lock and repeated the process of lifting the gate paddle. He had guessed that Mr Tripsy was not an experienced canal sailor. So the lock keeper opened the bottom paddle of the lock gate by about twelve centimetres.

It was not a big gap but Mr Tripsy got a shock when the jet of water spurted out from the gate, not quite splashing over the bow of Wave Crest.

The big difference now, was the fact that Mr Tripsy and Wave Crest, were being lifted up by the water inside the lock. When the water levels were equal, Mr Tripsy started the engine and gingerly eased his way out of the lock, waving his thanks to the lock keeper.

Gee, he thought, *I'm glad he did that for me.*

'Still, I think I could handle it ok if I had to do it,'

Flapjax, who as usual, had slumbered through most of the excitement but had been jolted to the land of the living by the tossing about, gave a snort. *Here we go again.*

With the lock safely behind him, Mr Tripsy decided to keep an eye out for somewhere to moor and maybe have a bite to eat.

Chapter 6

Mr Tripsy was glad that no one else was using this stretch of the canal. He decided to experiment with the boat controls. *A bit of practice won't do any harm,* he told himself.

So, after a quick look forward and aft (backwards to landlubbers), he pushed the throttle forward three notches. Wave Crest responded with a jerk and within moments was racing, well moving quite fast for a cabin cruiser along the canal.

Actually there was a speed limit of four knots, which is similar to a fast walking pace and Mr Tripsy felt he was doing better than that. He began to gently ease the steering wheel to and fro and Wave Crest began to zigzag through the water. 'Hey! This is fantastic,' he yelled and pushed the throttle up another two notches.

As the boat picked up more speed a large bow wave curled to the canal banks and the wash splashed over the towpath and a huge creamy wake streamed behind Wave Crest.

Then Mr Tripsy began to feel a bit queasy. The boat was surging from side to side and getting nearer and nearer to the stone edged canal banks. He gripped the steering wheel harder and tried to keep to the centre of the canal.

I don't think this was a good idea, he thought, *I need to slow down.* So, holding his breath, he reached over and pulled the throttle right back, remembering just in time to also put the clutch into neutral.

The roar of the engine died down and Wave Crest began to slow.

Phew! That was a bit hairy, thought a rather subdued Mr Tripsy. Then he got the fright of his life. About five hundred metres ahead was a large unusually shaped bridge.

'My Giddy Aunt! Look at that!' he cried. 'Thank goodness I slowed down.'

Then he remembered that this peculiar bridge was actually a lift bridge. There was no room to go underneath. The procedure was for canal users to use their hooter, so as to alert the bridge keeper if he had not already spotted them.

Where is that hooter button? He looked all over the control panel. Then he spotted it and pressed it twice. He heard a loud 'Toot! Toot!' sound above his head and the bridge began to lift up, stopping when it was completely upright.

So Mr Tripsy engaged the engine and slowly sailed through the gap left by the uplifted bridge. As he did so, he saw the bridge keeper in his little cabin waving at him. He was about to wave back when he thought he heard the words *idiot* and *not so fast.* He blushed and looked away, knowing he had behaved

in an irresponsible manner and sailed on.

About half an hour later he spotted a sign, The Wharf Tavern – 1 mile. *About time,* he thought.

About 10 minutes later, Mr Tripsy was passing a couple of long narrow boats and a cabin cruiser moored alongside the towpath, which passed by the Wharf Tavern, a small thatched building set back from the canal, with a group of picnic tables in a beer garden.

Easing the throttle back to idle, he moved the clutch to reverse and then gave a quick burst of power to the engine. The propeller went backwards and slowed the boat enough for him to rush forward and throw the bowline to a friendly guy on the towpath, who quickly tied it to a mooring post.

'Thanks!' called Mr Tripsy, as he made his way to the stern and hopping onto to the towpath, made fast the stern line. 'It's a bit awkward when you are on your own.'

'No problem,' replied the man. 'Glad to give a hand.'

Jumping back into the boat, Mr Tripsy went to the galley and opened the fridge and took out a carton of Kit milk, a bottle of coke and a packet of sandwiches. Then, from the cupboard above the small cooker, he got Flapjax's bowl and a handful of Fishio sticks. Putting everything in an old plastic shopping bag, he turned and called to Flapjax, who was still sprawled on the ledge above the steering wheel.

'Fishio's! Fishio's!'

With a loud meow, Flapjax jumped down and ran up to Mr Tripsy.

'Hang on! Hang on!' said Mr Tripsy with a grin. 'We're going to use one of the picnic tables.'

So after making sure the cabin door was safely locked, he picked up Flapjax after fixing a lead to him and put him on the towpath and then climbed up too.

They walked over to the Wharf Tavern and went into the beer garden. There were half a dozen picnic tables set among some cherry trees, two of them occupied. Mr Tripsy led Flapjax to one next to one of the cherry trees.

'Now then, let's get you sorted.' Taking out the Kit milk carton and Flapjax's bowl, he filled it with some milk and placed it on the grassy ground. Flapjax was at the bowl like flash and was lapping the milk with gusto when a brown furry ball rushed up, snapping and snarling. It was the small dog from the narrow boat that had been at the marina and the boat lift.

Flapjax stopped drinking and taking one look at the dog, ran to the cherry tree and raced up its trunk and crouched in the top branches, hissing with rage.

'Tiger! Tiger! Come here! Now!' It was the red-headed man and he was smiling. 'Don't worry, Tiger is only playing, aren't you?'

Tiger was at the bottom of the cherry tree jumping up and barking in a yapping sort of way.

'I think you should have your dog under control and on a lead,' said Mr Tripsy calmly.

'Is that so,' replied the red-headed man in a loud voice. 'And why have you brought a cat. You know plenty of people bring dogs to places like this.'

'Yes and they are well controlled, not like your dog,' said Mr Tripsy heatedly.

'I'm not stopping here to argue with you,' spluttered the man. 'Come on Tiger! Now! The tone of voice made Tiger stop barking and he ran over, tail down and with a little whimper.

As the red-headed man stomped off, Mr Tripsy coaxed Flapjax down by waving a couple of Fishio sticks at him.

Still feeling annoyed by the incident, Mr Tripsy ate

his sandwiches and finished his coke as quickly as he could. Then as soon as Flapjax had finished his meal, they went back to the boat.

Chapter 7

Mr Tripsy was fuming as he led Flapjax into Wave Crest's cabin. 'That guy is going to get it good and proper if he crosses me one more time this week.'

He grabbed a can of cider from the fridge and sat down on the bench seat. He took a big swig. 'Did I need that. How I kept my temper I don't know.'

He looked across at Flapjax who seemed unperturbed by the kerfuffle and was quietly grooming himself on top of the cockpit control panel. Finishing his drink, he tossed the empty can into his waste bin and said, 'I think I'll have an early night. What with one thing and another, it's been quite a day.'

So, leaving a bowl of water for Flapjax, he went into the forward cabin's bathroom to do his teeth and his other ablutions. After a last check to see if the boat's doors were locked, he gave Flapjax a pat and entered his cabin. He tried listening to his iPod for a few minutes but soon gave up. Switching off the light, he dropped off to sleep more or less immediately.

Chapter 8

The next morning, feeling better for a good nights sleep, Mr Tripsy had his breakfast as Flapjax scoffed his Fishio's and lapped up a bowl of Kit milk.

After dumping his dishes and cutlery in the sink and a quick tidy up, he grabbed the waste bin bag of rubbish, plus the cat litter tray bag and jumped across to the towpath and strolled along it to the large dump-it bin, which was by the path to the Wharf Tavern. Throwing in his two bags, Mr Tripsy then went back for Flapjax.

Flapjax was standing on the cockpit control panel looking anxiously through the windscreen and when Mr Tripsy opened the cabin door, he ran out and jumped onto the towpath.

'Hey! Come back, you little scamp,' shouted Mr Tripsy.

Taking no notice, Flapjax ran down the towpath towards the narrow boats moored there.

Sitting on top of one, was the brown Yorkshire terrier who had terrorized Flapjax the night before.

Flapjax raced to the narrow boat and jumped on top of one of its mooring bollards. Arching his back he gave a loud hiss.

The Yorkshire terrier jerked its head round and leapt up, yapping as noisily as it could.

Flapjax hissed again.

With a snarl of rage, the dog rushed along the top of the narrow boat and jumped towards Flapjax. Unfortunately, being a tiny dog he couldn't jump as far as he thought. The gap between the narrow boat and the towpath was just too wide.

'Splash!'

The Yorkshire terrier surfaced in the canal water, paddling round in tiny circles, yapping and whining.

'What the …..! What the devils going on!' The red-headed man stumbled out of the narrow boat cabin, wearing just a pair of shorts and half of his face covered in shaving soap.

'Tiger! Tiger! How the .... did you get there?' he yelled as he looked over the stern of his boat. Then he jumped into the canal. 'My God, the water's freezing,' he gasped as he reached out to grab hold of his dog. Of course Tiger wasn't having any of it. He paddled away.

'You little   .... !' shouted the red-haired man. 'Come back here.'

Mr Tripsy had watched in amazement as the red-haired man jumped into the canal. Quick as a flash he turned round and ran to an emergency life-buoy stand and grabbed it. Running back to the canal side he threw it into the water.

Shivering in the cold water, the red-haired man eagerly grabbed hold of the life-buoy and Mr Tripsy having held on to his end of the line, pulled him towards the towpath and hauled him out of the canal.

The partner of the red-headed man rushed up and wrapped him in a large bath robe. 'Are you all right,' she asked anxiously.

He nodded, still shaken by the unexpected coldness of the canal. Shivering violently he was led back to his narrow boat.

Meanwhile, the Yorkshire terrier, had paddled its way to a nearby boat launching ramp and after shaking its fur dry had slunk towards the narrow boat's gang plank and crept quietly aboard.

By now several people had gathered round to gawk and stare at the goings on. So Mr Tripsy decided to go back to his boat, especially as Flapjax had already started to walk back in a way which signified he knew that he was now equal with the dog.

Chapter 9

Once on board, Mr Tripsy picked up his map of the canal system off the control panel and sitting down began to plan for the next stage of his trip. He idly watched Flapjax jump up onto the control panel ledge, which he seemed to have claimed as his own.

Mr Tripsy had been studying the map for nearly half an hour when a 'Toot! Toot!' made him jump. Looking through the side window he saw a narrow boat alongside. Going on deck he saw it was the red-headed man's boat and he was waving to Mr Tripsy.

'I just wanted to say thanks for helping me when I was in the canal,' he shouted across to Mr Tripsy, 'And to give you this.' He was holding a bottle of red wine and then said. 'Grab hold of it and thanks again.'

Mr Tripsy was quite amazed at how friendly the man was. 'Ermm. I... I... there's no need to....'

'Grab it man. We haven't all day. We're just about to leave.'

'Well if you insist,' said Mr Tripsy. 'Thanks very much.'

'My pleasure.'

The red-headed man then pushed the throttle forward and the narrow boat eased away down the canal with a couple more 'Toot! Toots!'

'Well, that was a surprise', said Mr Tripsy as he went down to the cabin and put the bottle of wine by the fridge. 'You can never tell what some people will do next.'

He looked across to Flapjax, lying on the cockpit control panel ledge quietly grooming himself.

'I noticed that 'Tiger' wasn't around. I bet he has him on a lead for the rest their holiday. OK then. Let's get started.'

He put the map back on the control panel and

went outside. Hopping onto the towpath he untied the fore (bow) and aft mooring lines, then jumped back aboard Wave Crest and started the engine.

Cruising along, listening to his iPod through a pair of earbuds, time passed quickly but enjoyably.

Stopping for a break, he moored by a small flash cum nature reserve. After a drink of chilled cider and seeing to Flapjax, he went for a stroll in it, though only after making sure to fix a lead on Flapjax.

The path zig-zagged between a copse of trees and then followed the pond's edge. Tall bull-rushes and other reeds lined it in thick clumps. A moorhen popped out of one of the clumps of reeds and got the fright of its life when Flapjax lunged at it. *Good job I brought the lead,* thought Mr Tripsy.

A short time later, it was Flapjax who was at the receiving end. Pulling on his lead, Flapjax went round an old tree log, which was blocking the path.

With a loud Honk! Honk! a fully grown Canada goose stood up and began to flap its large wings. Then hissing angrily, it charged at Flapjax.

With a screech of alarm Flapjax turned tail and ran back towards Mr Tripsy, who also thought it a good idea to retreat.

'I think it's time to go back anyway,' he said, glad to lead the way back to the boat.

Settled once again in Wave Crest, Mr Tripsy sailed along the canal, marvelling at how quiet it was. Then he realized why there was so little boat traffic. Following a curve in the canal he was astonished to see several locks going up the side of a hill. There was a queue of six boats waiting to go up.

'I know what it is,' he said. 'They're staircase locks.' *(To go high up a hill, a canal boat had to proceed through a series of connected locks called a flight. The most famous has a flight of thirty locks).*

To go through the locks was just like before but it took much longer. During the next couple of hours he had to negotiate a series of five locks. Fortunately, the lock keepers were really helpful as always and there were plenty of volunteers from the other boats ready to help as well.

Later that afternoon Mr Tripsy decided to moor and call it a day. He was knackered, to coin a phrase. *It's practice, that's all you need, plenty of practice,* he told himself. *I'll feel better tomorrow.*

As before, he found a handy mooring spot near a pub. Which came first, he thought, the canal or the pub. Who cares, let's put our feet up.

Quickly tying his mooring lines, he fed Flapjax and after a hot drink and a sandwich, flopped on the bench seat and fell asleep.

Chapter 10

Mr Tripsy woke up with a start. 'What time is it?' he mumbled. The boat cabin was dark. He realized that he was still in the main cabin, lying on the bench seat. *Ugh! I'm stiff all over.* He stood up and switched the cabin lights on. His watch showed that it was nearly ten o'clock. *I don't believe it. Ten o'clock. It can't be.* A sound made him look round. Flapjax was at the cabin door, mewing, obviously wanting to go out.

'Sorry! Flapjax. I must have flaked out,' he said in a tired voice. 'Evidently I'm not as fit as I thought I was. Hang on, I'll be with you in a minute.' Mr Tripsy went to the sink and got a glass of water.

He drank it greedily. 'Ah! That's better. Lets go then,' he said, opening the cabin door. Flapjax raced through and jumped onto the towpath.

'Wait for me you little devil. Wait for me.' He had to stop for a moment to pick up Flapjax's lead. By the time he had got to the towpath Flapjax had disappeared.

'Blast! Where has he got to?' In the glow of the pub's illuminated sign, Mr Tripsy saw a hedgerow lining the towpath parallel with the canal. *He must have gone in there, so* jumping back down onto Wave Crest's deck he rushed into the cabin and switched on the lights. Going over to the control panel he grabbed the torch, which hung from a plastic hook right next to it.

Once he was back on the towpath he switched on the torch and went through a large hole in the hedge and followed a well-trodden path. *Aha,* he thought. *Some people don't like paying for toilets. I'd better watch where I step.*

A moment or two later, Mr Tripsy heard a bark. *Funny, that doesn't sound like a dog.*

He went on a few more metres and then stopped. In a small clearing amongst the bushes, his torchlight picked out an amazing sight. Flapjax was crouched down next to a large dead bird. It looked like a male pheasant, its radiant feathers reflected in the torchlight. Facing Flapjax and the bird was a fox, (a vixen, Mr Tripsy surmised, because of that funny bark he had heard a few minutes before).

The fox turned and looked at Mr Tripsy, its eyes reflecting like small jewels in the torchlight. It opened its mouth wide, as though yawning and then, without a sound, slunk away through the bushes.

'Flapjax!' cried Mr Tripsy, making sure not to point the torch directly at him. 'Fishio's! Fishio's!'

Jerking his head round, Flapjax stood up and reluctantly left the dead pheasant. He walked slowly over to Mr Tripsy and mewed.

Thank goodness I had some in my pocket. 'Here you are,' said a relieved Mr Tripsy, giving a couple of Fishio sticks to Flapjax. Then he put the lead round his neck whilst he was feeding on them.

It only took a minute or two to get back to the canal towpath and back on the boat.

Mr Tripsy then filled Flapjax's bowl with some Kit milk. 'Whilst you're guzzling that, I'm going to the pub for a take-away.'

Half an hour later, a much happier Mr Tripsy cleared away his take-away boxes and making sure that Flapjax had finished off his grilled fish steak sat down and toasted the red-headed man again with his third glass of red wine.

Chapter 11

Rather later than he had intended, Mr Tripsy got up and drew back the cabin window curtain. It was raining. Well a light drizzle really. 'Well, I suppose it had to rain sometime,' he muttered to himself.

After a quick shower, he rustled up some breakfast, noticing that he needed to get some more fresh food and milk.

Flapjax as usual, scoffed his Kit milk and Fishio sticks in record time and was prowling up and down the cabin.

Mr Tripsy looked at him and smiled. 'Got cabin fever have you old sport. Don't worry we'll be outside in a minute or two.'

He had seen a small shop further down the towpath the previous night when he had called in the pub for his take-away. *The Fox and Pheasant,* he had noticed on the sign. *Now why does that ring a bell,* he thought. Then he remembered going into the bushes after Flapjax and seeing a fox and a dead pheasant. *My Giddy Aunt, what a flipping coincidence.*

So after fixing a lead on Flapjax (no racing off this morning) he walked down the towpath to the shop.

It was a general store providing a much needed service to the passing canal boats. Shops are few and far between along the canals and are much appreciated. This one also provided a post box.

'Oh, Oh, that reminds me,' said Mr Tripsy, eyeing the post box. I need to get a postcard and send it off today before I get into trouble.' He had promised his girlfriend, (well maybe that was a bit strong. They had only been out a few times) to send a card. Umm, maybe I shouldn't have left my mobile in the car.

It was quiet in the shop, the morning rush being over. The shop assistant by the till wished him a good-morning and passed him a shopping basket.

'Could be better,' replied Mr Tripsy with a smile. 'Is it ok to bring in my pet cat?'

'Well, seeing it's so quiet, and if you make it quick,' the shop assistant said.

Trying to oblige, Mr Tripsy whipped round the tiny shop as fast as he could. He managed to get everything he wanted, including a nice canal scene postcard and a book of postage stamps.

At the cash till, the shop assistant helped to bag the items Mr Tripsy had bought and said in a low voice, 'If you are going through Dywoman Tunnel take care. Strange things have been seen in there.'

Mr Tripsy didn't know what to say, so he said politely, 'Thanks, I'll bear it in mind. Bye.'

Beside the shop entrance was a wooden bench, so Mr Tripsy tied one end of Flapjax's lead to it and sat down to write his postcard. A short time later, after posting it he walked back to his boat thinking what on earth was that assistant talking about.

Back in the boat he took off his wet anorak, draping it over the end of the bench seat to dry, made a cup of coffee and gave Flapjax another bowl of Kit milk.

Chapter 12

The weather had if anything got worse. A light mist was covering the surface of the canal like a silver-grey blanket. 'Well, there's no point in staying here,' said Mr Tripsy firmly. 'We might as well go on.'

So slipping on his anorak, he went to untie the fore and aft mooring lines. Rubbing his hands, he returned to the main cabin. 'It's flipping freezing out there,' he complained and threw his anorak onto the bench seat.

Flapjax, sprawled on top of the control panel as usual, turned his head and looked pitifully at Mr Tripsy as though thinking, *Why don't you have fur like us cats. It's so simple.*

The next hour or so was a bit boring for Mr Tripsy. He could only see for about one hundred metres and that meant he had to travel at a much-reduced speed. 'I can crawl as fast as this,' he mumbled in a frustrated voice.

Then out of the gloom came a sign, Dywoman Tunnel – Take care.

The tunnel entrance looked rather forbidding. Not much higher than the top of Wave Crest's cabin, the dark entrance with the swirling mist wafting in and out, as though a giant was breathing through its mouth, was definitely scary.

He stopped the engine and Wave Crest drifted slowly towards the mouth of the tunnel. It was eerily quiet. No bird song, nothing. The mist seemed to be getting thicker and even inside the boat the air suddenly got colder.

Mr Tripsy gave a shudder and thought, *This is ridiculous. I'm going on.*

Starting the engine again, he eased the throttle forward one notch and slowly entered the tunnel. After about twenty metres, it was completely dark.

'Blast! I forgot about the lights,' said an exasperated Mr Tripsy, as he switched on the cabin lights and a forward spotlight.

Now he could see that the towpath looked dangerous to walk on. It was damp and slippery from water oozing and dripping from cracks in the wall and roof. The mist seemed to hover just above the canal water, swirling in small clouds as the boat slowly edged forward.

'Jeez!' he exclaimed, 'How on earth did they manage in the old days. Fancy going through here by candle light.'

Without any warning the mist suddenly got so thick he could hardly see past the bow of Wave Crest and it went as cold as ice. 'What the heck's happening,' he cried in an alarmed voice.

Then Flapjax jumped up with a hiss and the fur on his back stood up like tiny spikes. With another hiss and a screech, he leapt down off the control panel and ran to his basket and stood stock still, rigid with fear.

Mr Tripsy suddenly noticed he was gripping the steering wheel so tight his knuckles were white. Then before he could react to Flapjax's problem, he heard a voice from outside the cabin. The muffled echo of the boat's engine made it hard for him to make out what was being said, so he slid open the side window.

'I want me ma, I want me ma,' a sobbing voice came from the direction of the towpath a few metres ahead of the boat. It sounded like a small child.

Then a sudden swirl of air cleared a patch of mist, enough for Mr Tripsy to see a small girl sitting on the damp towpath, sobbing her little heart out.

She seemed to be dressed in a long, dark-grey, old-fashioned frock with a dirty white apron tied to the front and long-laced leather boots.

Before Mr Tripsy could say or do anything the mist cleared again and to his amazement he saw another canal tunnel leading away to his right. Then Flapjax, squalling like mad, ran back to the control panel and jumped up to his usual place and then sat there, quietly staring into the mist.

The mist swirled again and Mr Tripsy suddenly realized that he could only hear the sound of the boat's engine. There was no sign or sound of the little girl. What's more he could no longer see the other canal tunnel.

Loosening his grip on the steering wheel Mr Tripsy let out a gasp. He had been holding his breath for goodness knows how long. 'What the hell was all that about,' he said in a wondering tone. 'No more wine for me.' Then he thought. *If I told anyone about what I thought I saw, they'd think I was a nut case.*

Just then he saw the end of the tunnel and with a great sigh of relief sailed into the open air and with luck, a place to moor.

Chapter 13

He did find a mooring spot not too far along the canal from the tunnel, next to an elderly couple in a smart, new looking narrow boat.

After fixing the mooring lines, Mr Tripsy took Flapjax for a run along the towpath. The drizzle had stopped and a watery sun was trying to poke through the leaden clouds.

Sloshing through a series of muddy puddles, he decided to call it a day and calling Flapjax, returned to the boat for something to eat.

Actually, he was still wound up thinking about what had happened in the tunnel. He still couldn't believe he had seen a ghost like figure, let alone another canal inside that tunnel. *There must be a rational explanation,* he thought.

In a dreamlike state he had a meal and somehow remembered to feed Flapjax, who after he had finished, bagged his place on the control panel ledge and began his catnap.

By now the sun had broken through and it was quite pleasant and warm outside, so Mr Tripsy dug out a folding camp chair and went to sit on the towpath.

He leaned back in his chair and stretched out his legs and took a long drink from a can of cider. *Aah, that's more like it, he* thought. Then he heard the couple on the next boat talking. He couldn't help it, as their boat window was open.

'Well there must be something in it Eddie. I mean, how many people have we heard this week talking about the terrible accident that happened in that tunnel, just up yonder.'

'Accident. No one is sure if it wasn't sommit else like.'

'What do mean, Eddie?'

'Well, I did hear someone say that some kind of skull-duggery took place.'

'Ooooh, Eddy, what happened?'

'I believe it was about one narrow boat trying to jump the queue. In those days, don't forget we're talking about one hundred and sixty odd years ago, if you weren't sharp, you could loose a cargo. That meant your family went hungry for a while. I read somewhere, it was dog eat dog.'

'What's that, Eddie?'

'Well, I believe some of the canal folk of that time would do something nasty to another competitor, like setting free the tow-horse or even worse, poisoning it.'

'I say Eddie, is that what happened here?'

'Course not. It had to be something really bad to happen for the story to last as long as it has.'

'Ooooh, Eddie, go on and tell me.'

'Its not gospel, you know. It's just what I picked up last night in the pub. You know. You had a headache remember and I went out for a jar so as to give you a break from me, like. Anyway, a couple of locals were talking about the tunnel and they reckon that there was a murder.'

'Ooooh Eddie, I don't think I want to know now.'

'Now lass, you asked and I'm going to tell you. It won't take long, I promise. Apparently, a narrow boat crewed by a widow and her small daughter, somehow got in front of a boat crewed by a nasty piece of work called Knuckles Janty. It was said he was furious at being taken for a ride, especially by a woman.

The story goes that he followed her into the tunnel and only he came out. He claimed that he saw her going into a side tunnel on the right and not knowing where it went, stayed on the left and never saw her again. The Peelers were called (police) and they searched his boat and found bloodstains next to the tiller. They also found a shawl which friends of the widow said could be hers.

The Peelers took him to Nantwich jail and he was later found hanging in his cell. People said that proved he murdered the widow and her small daughter.'

'Ooooh Eddie, How horrible.'

'The strange thing though, is the fact they never found the narrow boat or the bodies. And over the years, lots of people passing through Dywoman's Tunnel, have said they have seen a little girl dressed in old fashioned clothes and some *claim to have seen a side tunnel as well'.*

'I say Eddie, would you close that window please? It seems to be getting a bit chilly.'

Mr Tripsy slowly sat up in his chair. He had slunk down in it, whilst listening to the story. He shivered and stood up. *Serves you right for listening to other people's conversations.*

Nothing good ever comes from it, he thought as he folded his chair and went aboard Wave Crest.

Chapter 14

After breakfast, Mr Tripsy looked around the cabin and thought, *it's a new day and what's done is done. Now that's what I call a good motto.*

Having made up his mind, he felt much better and he wandered over to the control panel and picked up his canal map and began to plan the day's trip.

'Not nine,' he said aloud. He studied the map more closely. There was no mistake. The next stretch of the canal had nine single locks each about a mile apart and each one had to be opened by the boat crew themselves. No lock keepers to help. 'Blast, it'll take me ages to get through them if no one else is there.'

The side effect of not having any other crew was now becoming obvious. He then gave a small laugh, thinking of all the exercise he was going to get, especially using the windlass. 'My poor aching back,' he said, laughing again.

Four hours later, he wasn't laughing. He had just moored by one of the canal's wayside cafes and was walking stiffly towards it.

'Having a bad day?' It was the red-headed man and he was just leaving. Pulling on his lead was Tiger, who came nearer to sniff at Mr Tripsy's ankles.

'Er, well actually I'm a little stiff. The locks you know.'

'Ha, didn't you bring your little helper. My partner is as strong as an ox. Well she should be the number of locks we've been through. As captain you have to skipper the boat, the crew do the heavy stuff, right. Heh, Heh.'

'Well, I… I… didn't realize it was so complicated sailing on a canal.'

'Complicated, complicated. Delegate man, delegate. That's what I do. It's been a doddle so far, well, apart from that little mishap when I went into the canal.'

'I see what you mean,' said Mr Tripsy trying to edge away. Tiger had started to pull at his shoelaces.

'Oh don't mind him, he's just being friendly. Tiger stop that! Sorry, he does get carried away sometimes. Tiger, come here.'

'I must go,' said Mr Tripsy, bending down to pull Tiger off his ankle. Bye.'

'Oh. OK!' If you're going to the aqueduct we might see you there. Watch your back now, ha, ha. Cheers for now. Come on Tiger. Come on.'

'What a ……,' thought Mr Tripsy as he entered the café. He joined the queue and ordered sausage, egg and chips with baked beans, tea and a cup cake. *Have to be quick Flapjax needs to be fed as well.*

Twenty minutes later, feeling quite human once

more, he went back to the boat, his back still aching a bit. He did a bit of tidying up whilst Flapjax had something to eat. There was usually a bowl of water by his basket but Mr Tripsy got the carton of Kit milk out as well.

After a hot shower, which did wonders for his aching back, he sorted out the mooring lines and got ready to start the engine.

Having picked up the routine by now, Flapjax was already sitting on his ledge, looking wistfully through the windscreen at a bevy of ducks swarming round a narrow boat, as a small child threw pieces of bread into the water. His ears pricked forward as the sound of *'Quack' 'Quack', 'Quack' 'Quack',* drifted in through the open side window.

'OK! Lets go,' said Mr Tripsy cheerfully, as he engaged the throttle and Wave Crest surged forward nice and smoothly. *Not bad, not bad at all,* he thought, *I must be getting used to it now.*

One hour later the countryside began to change. The canal had passed through a rather flat valley with little scenic interest and was approaching a series of hills. 'Blast!' said Mr Tripsy in an annoyed voice, 'I hope it's not a staircase lock, not with the state my back's in.'

As Wave Crest followed the curve of the canal, Mr Tripsy got quite a shock. A steep valley appeared in front of the boat and most of it was below the level of the canal.

'My Giddy Aunt!' cried Mr Tripsy in surprise. 'How the heck do we get down to that valley? We don't need a staircase lock. We need an escalator.'

Then he saw an amazing sight. The canal was going straight across the valley, at least thirty metres in the air. *This must be an aqueduct.*

There must have been about ten stone arches, carrying a giant iron trough filled with the water of

the canal.

'This is fantastic, super. Err, I hope I don't fall off.' Mr Tripsy suddenly felt a shiver go down his spine.

'Flapjax, Flpajax just look at that.'

Wave Crest was now in the middle of the aqueduct.

Flapjax sat up and looked out of the side window. All he saw was space, no ground, just the sky. *What's all the fuss about? There's nothing there. Boring.* And he went back to sleep.

Mr Tripsy gave a shudder as he looked again through the side window. Being higher up than Flapjax, he was able to see right over the side of the aqueduct. In fact if he reached out he could actually touch it. There was nothing between it and the ground thirty metres below. *Don't look down. Don't look down*, he told himself.

He didn't realize he was sweating until he reached the end of the aqueduct. *Well, that was quite something. I wouldn't say great. It scared me to death but it was definitely something to experience.*

There was a mooring place not far from the aqueduct and Mr Tripsy made a beeline for it. Once moored up, he grabbed a can of cider from the fridge and pressed the ice-cool can to his forehead for a minute, then took a big swig. *Ah! Just what I wanted.*

Then he collapsed on the bench settee and looked at Flapjax. 'Don't say anything. Don't you dare say anything.'

Flapjax flicked his tail, as though *to say, As if I would.*

Chapter 15

Mr Tripsy was glad that he had decided to call it a day that afternoon. The last day or so had been more exhausting than he had realized, both mentally and physically.

A good lie-in was unfortunately spoilt when several seagulls descended on the front of Wave Crest's bow to fight over the scraps from a boat's rubbish bin bag. One of them had picked up a manky looking piece of chicken and had carried it to the Wave Crest. Hence the screeching and squalling.

Mr Tripsy appeared bleary eyed in the main cabin. There was no point in staying in bed with that racket. Then he had an idea.

Flapjax was standing on his ledge, eyes glued to the windscreen watching the gulls, his tail swishing to and fro.

He opened the cabin door. Flapjax was out like a rocket and of course the gulls took off when they saw the bounding cat coming towards them.

Peace reigned. 'Well done, Flapjax, come and get your Fishio sticks.'

Then he saw the mess that the gulls had left on the front deck of Wave Crest. White on white could still be seen and if left would damage the paint work. *That's all I need. A pile of bird muck to clean up before breakfast.*

Flapjax wandered in from the deck and made for his basket and the plate of Fishio sticks lying next to it and began feeding.

Waiting for the kettle to boil, Mr Tripsy got out a bowl and poured in some Dettol and grabbed hold of an old rag. As soon as the water was hot enough he mixed it with the Dettol and carried the bowl out onto the deck, chuntering. 'Jeez, the things you have to do on a boat.'

Ten minutes later, having disposed of the dirty rag and washed out the bowl he had a quick shower and got dressed. He was too annoyed to have breakfast, making do with just a glass of orange juice.

Today, he had decided, *he would make a trip along the River Trent.* He had read that something special took place on it, but he had forgotten what it was. There was a short 'cutting' not too far away, which led to a connecting junction lock with the river.

A couple passing by at that moment, untied his mooring lines and after a thank you, Mr Tripsy started the boat's engine, that being the cue for Flapjax to resume his favourite sailing position i.e. on his ledge above the control panel.

They were soon cruising along the canal and he began to relax. He had fixed his iPod to his belt and so after putting his earbuds on, began to listen to the Nashville Bluegrass Band and was soon tapping his feet to the beat of the music.

After negotiating four different locks, Mr Tripsy arrived at the connecting junction lock and joined a queue of three narrow boats waiting to pass through. It gave him time to make a sandwich and have a cup of coffee. The weather was holding up quite well and Mr Tripsy took advantage by putting his folding camp chair on the bow deck (there was just enough room) and was just relaxing and sunning himself whilst waiting his turn to enter the lock, when he was interrupted by a shout.

'Hi, how are you doing?' It was the red-headed man and he was carrying two cans of lager. 'Here, catch,' he said throwing one to Mr Tripsy, who making a grab, just managed to catch hold of it without falling out of his chair.

'You wouldn't believe what happened to us yesterday,' continued the man as he put a foot on Wave Crest's foredeck and took a drink from his can.

Mr Tripsy opened his and taking a drink, acknowledged the nod from his new found 'friend.'

'We were passing through Harefield Tunnel; you know the one that has a history of strange goings on. I mean, most of the canal tunnels are supposed to be haunted or have something odd about them, that is, if you believe in old wives tales. Anyway, we were tootling along through this tunnel, when Tiger, you know, my dog.'

Only too well, thought Mr Tripsy.

'Well, he started yapping like mad. I mean it's kinda spooky at the best of times, isn't it, going through a pitch black tunnel with only a spotlight and your cabin lights on.'

Mr Tripsy nodded; he quite understood that all right.

Well. I still can't believe what happened. I saw this shaggy creature. It was grunting or moaning and I thought it looked kinda monkey like but wasn't, if you know what I mean.'

'Err, not really,' muttered Mr Tripsy but intrigued all the same.

'Of course,' the man went on, 'Tiger went 'ape,' no pun intended, running up and down the roof of our boat. My partner took one look at the bright, staring eyes of this thing and practically fell down into our cabin, shrieking. *For God's sake, don't let it get on board!*

'Yeah! The eyes were shining. I suppose they might have been reflecting back the boats light, but they did seem different somehow. For instance they seemed to be a funny colour, not like say, the way cats eyes reflect light.

Anyway. It was shuffling along the towpath and making this groaning noise, as it came towards us, so I went straight into reverse, I damn nearly broke the engine's clutch.

Fortunately, no one was behind us and I made it

55

back to the mooring place and watched and waited but the thing never came out.'

'Maybe it went back the other way,' said a transfixed Mr Tripsy.

'Yeah! But another narrow boat came out not too long after, from the other end of the tunnel and as it passed me I asked the skipper if he had seen anything strange whilst he was passing through. He said he hadn't.'

Thinking for a moment the man said, 'Tiger really went hysterical for a time, you know. He must have sensed something abnormal. Animals are like that aren't they?'

He looked over at Mr Tripsy, 'Something funny happened in that tunnel, as sure as I'm standing here.'

'I agree with you that animals can sense things we can't,' said Mr Tripsy. 'I sometimes think my cat has a sixth sense though to be honest, I think most of these type of stories have a rational explanation.'

'Yeah! Well, that maybe so but I saw what I saw and so did my partner and dog. Gee! I still feel funny about it now. Anyway, we waited until another boat turned up to go through the tunnel and we followed them. I don't mind telling you. I was glad of their company.

Well, I'd better be going. It looks as if the lock is ready for us. I hope you didn't mind me offloading this onto you. It sure makes me feel better getting it off my chest. Thanks for listening and for not making any funny cracks about my mental health. See you.'

'Oh! Right. Bye and thanks for the drink,' said a bemused Mr Tripsy.

Chapter 16

It took only three quarters of an hour to reach the end of the cutting and pass though into the River Trent. It was much wider than the River Weaver and the current stronger, so Mr Tripsy had to increase the boat's speed to keep control of the rudder. There was more boat traffic as well, something Mr Tripsy had not really encountered before so he was a little anxious to begin with.

He learnt to keep a good lookout and to make the necessary course adjustments in good time. He quickly settled into the rhythm and was soon enjoying the change from canal sailing.

As he travelled downriver it became wider and wider, so much so that Mr Tripsy began to feel a bit nervous. Then, a *toot, toot,* made him jump. A narrow boat was overtaking him. He looked over and saw the red-headed man grinning at him.

'I thought it was you,' the man shouted across. 'Do you usually block other boats' right of way?'

'It's not me, it's you who is on the wrong side of the river,' Mr Tripsy shouted back.

With a casual wave from the skipper, the narrow boat surged ahead and raced away.

He's asking for trouble, thought Mr Tripsy as he looked at the narrow boat disappearing into the distance round a bend in the river.

Settling down once again to the serious business of boat navigation, he glanced at the familiar, slumbering form of Flapjax, lying comfortably on his ledge above the steering wheel. *Not a bad life,* he thought, *all mod cons, food on demand and somebody to blame if anything goes wrong.*

A few minutes later, he rounded the bend and noticed that the river straightened out for the best part of a mile (about 1600 metres).

Then in the far distance something odd was happening. A dark line had formed right across the river. Leaning across to the side window, Mr Tripsy grabbed hold of the binoculars hanging there from a hook.

Holding the steering wheel with one hand he quickly focused the binoculars and gave a loud gasp. 'I don't believe it. What the hell is that?'

He pressed the binoculars closer to his eyes and looked again. There was no doubt about it. A giant wave, well at least a huge one was racing up river and in front of it obviously trying to outrun it was a narrow boat.

There was something familiar about it. Yes, he could see it now, a small dog running up and down the roof of the cabin. It was the narrow boat of the red-headed man. What on earth was he doing?

Then it clicked. He had remembered the article he had read about the River Trent, sometime last year. *At certain times of the year, a naturally occurring tidal wave like the Severn Bore, forms as the rising tide forces a large volume of water through a narrowing river channel.*

Jeez, this tidal wave or bore was happening now and it must be getting on for two metres high, thought Mr Tripsy *and it's getting nearer every second.*

'My God, What can I do. I've never seen one before let alone been in one.'

By now the narrow boat was fairly near and he could see what was happening without using the binoculars. The partner of the red-headed man had leant on the cabin roof and coaxed Tiger to come near enough for her to grab him. Mr Tripsy watched as they dropped down into the cabin.

Then every thing went to pot. For some reason the narrow boat suddenly slowed down and began to veer sideways.

The tidal bore rushed up and swamped the narrow boat. It disappeared in a cloud of spray.

'Oh! No!' cried Mr Tripsy, as he watched helplessly. Without thinking he pushed the gear stick all the way to full speed and Wave Crest responded like a willing horse and raced towards the stricken narrow boat.

By now the tidal bore had surged past the rocking and rolling narrow boat. *'At least it's still afloat,'* thought a relieved Mr Tripsy. Then he gave a gasp of alarm as the tidal bore loomed high above Wave Crest's deck and came down with a thunderous crash.

The wave smashed over the bow and into the windscreen. Flapjax gave a screech as he felt the boat tilt over and he jumped to the floor and ran to his basket. Mr Tripsy flinched and ducked down behind the control panel, desperately holding onto the steering wheel as Wave Crest's bow dipped under the weight of water smashing down, then with a shudder and a scream from the propeller which was now raised above the waterline, the boat punched through the tidal bore and settled into the relatively calm river behind it.

'Jeez! I never, ever, want to do that again,' exclaimed a grateful and much happier Mr Tripsy as he realized that the boat had come through undamaged.

Then he remembered the narrow boat. *'Oh My! Where is it, I hope they are alright,'* he thought anxiously. Then he saw the boat, about two hundred metres away. It was swirling round and round in the river current. It obviously had no working engine.

'Hey! Can you hear me,' a voice from the narrow boat called out. Then, 'I don't believe it; it's that bloke with the cat.'

Mr Tripsy poked his head out of the side window beside the steering wheel. 'Hi, do you need some help. I've a cat who is very good at catching fish.'

'Never mind the fish. Can you give us a tow. I stupidly burnt out the engine clutch trying to race the tidal bore. We haven't steerageway.'

In other words, Mr Clever has knackered up the boat engine, thought Mr Tripsy.

'No problem,' shouted Mr Tripsy, 'Except I can't leave the helm. I'm on my own, remember.'

'Ah, yes.' said the red-headed man. Then he called back. 'If I come on board your boat after I have fixed a tow-rope at my end, I will be able to attach it to your stern and then you would be able to tow me back to that marina further up river. Now that the tide has turned, your boat should be able to manage it easily.'

Mr Tripsy thought for a moment and called back. 'Good thinking. That should do it.'

So, after a few false manoeuvres, Mr Tripsy managed to get alongside the narrow boat and the tow-rope was soon attached to Wave Crest's stern.

A couple of hours later the narrow boat was safely moored in the marina's repair yard.

'We can't thank you enough,' the red-headed man said with a large smile. He was with his partner, as they all walked back to the spot where Wave Crest was moored. 'That was the hairiest thing we've ever been through.' His partner gave him such a look, as though to say. *Who's fault was it then?*

'Anyway,' he added, 'We'd like you to have this with our thanks.' He passed Mr Tripsy a wrapped parcel.

'Oh there's no need for that…. Well if you insist. Thank you very much,' said an embarrassed Mr Tripsy.

He waved goodbye as they went back into the marina and with a sigh, climbed aboard Wave Crest and a very warm welcome from Flapjax, who had decided that it was, if not tea time, definitely 'Fishio and Kit milk time.'

Once he had fed Flapjax, Mr Tripsy mentally made a note that he had to return Wave Crest back to the Western Flash Marina tomorrow. *Would he go on the canals again? He wasn't sure. Maybe, maybe not.*

He then made a coffee and munching on a chocolate biscuit and sitting on the bench settee, opened his parcel. It contained a large book. The title read, *'Ghostly Canal Stories.'*

Mr Tripsy paused, and he looked at the title again and frowned. *Who really knows, he thought. Did I see that little girl in that tunnel or is it all in my mind.*

He got up and walked over to the cockpit control panel and bent down to open the bottom drawer. He took out a small brown paper parcel and carefully opened it. *He looked down at the small child's, long-laced leather boot in his hand. It was all of a hundred and sixty odd years old and he had found it on the cabin floor, the morning after his trip through Dywoman Tunnel.*

The End

Printed in Germany
by Amazon Distribution
GmbH, Leipzig